Come On, Patsy

ATHENEUM

New York   1982

Come On,

Patsy

by Zilpha Keatley Snyder

pictures by Margot Zemach

Library of Congress Cataloging in Publication Data

Snyder, Zilpha Keatley.
  Come on, Patsy.

  SUMMARY: As Patsy and her friend walk to the park,
she gets talked into situations that always seem to
leave her the loser and a bit the worse for wear. But
her bossy friend loses, too.
  [1. Friendship—Fiction] I. Zemach, Margot, ill.
II. Title.
PZ7.S68522Co   [E]   81-10814
ISBN 0-689-30892-2   AACR2

Published simultaneously in Canada by
McClelland & Stewart, Ltd.
Text set by Linoprint Composition, New York City
Printed and bound by South China Printing Company, Hong Kong

Typography by Mary M. Ahern
First American Edition

Hi, Patsy. Do you want to play?
Want to go to the park?
I know a new way.

Come on, Patsy. What's wrong?
You don't have to ask.
We won't be gone long.

The first thing we do is jump
over this wire.

You should have jumped higher.

To get over the fence you just clumb up this tree.

9

Did you hurt your knee?

Now we tiptoe across the lawn.

No, that wasn't a growl.
It was only a yawn.

KEEP OF
THE
LAWN

See it was just a yawn.
Don't you worry.

I told you to hurry.

Don't cry, Patsy, you're all right.
There's a rip right here, but
he didn't bite.

Aren't you glad, Patsy,
that we came my way?
Now there's lots of time to play.

There's a line for the swings, Patsy.
Hurry, run fast. Patsy get up.
Do you want to be last?

I'm pushing hard, Patsy.
I'm making you fly.

Why didn't you say
you don't like to go high?

I know you can make it. I'll say
ready . . . set . . . go. . . . Oh, no!

Knock it off, Patsy.
Will you stop fussing please.
You're perfectly dry except up to
your knees.

21

I'm hungry, Patsy. Are you hungry too?
If I had some money, I'd buy one for you.

Well look at the money you had all the time.
Three nickles, six pennies, and look—
there's a dime!

Here you are, Patsy. Here's your share.

There is too some left.
Right down in there!

The merry-go-round, the merry-go-round.
Isn't it fun to go round and round.
Stop the merry-go-round. Stop it quick!

I didn't know it was making her sick.

We're almost home, Patsy.
Look. Here comes your dad.

Wow, I don't see why he had to
get mad.

Come on, Patsy.
Want to go play?

Now why in the world
is she acting that way?

Come on, Patsy!